CW01052142

Bigfoc

The Legend Behind. ...

Michael J. Egbert

Copyright © 2024 by Michael J. Egbert.

All rights reserved. Except as permitted under the U.S. Copyright Act of 1976. No part of this book may be reproduced, distributed, or transmitted in any form or by any means, electronic or mechanical, including photocopying, recording, or by any information storage, database, or retrieval system, without the prior written permission of the author.

The characters and events portrayed in this book are fictitious. Any similarity to real persons, living or dead, is coincidental and not intended by the author.

Print ISBN: 979-8-3303-6550-0

This book is dedicated to my children. May you always see the world for what it can be.

Every creature has a story to tell. However, some believe these stories are not worth listening to. This is an unfortunate abnormality found within the human brain. It occurs when one person believes that another is not worth their time. Regrettably, to these poor souls, such tales are worth less than the paper they're written on.

Some may consider this story to be an example of such an account. To them, thumbing through these pages would be an exercise in futility. Although, no story could be of greater worth than the one concerning the creature known as Bigfoot.

Like most mythical creatures, Bigfoot is misunderstood. He's been labeled a monster or even a thing of fiction. Some say he's a distant cousin to the Himalayan Yeti, but it's not his size nor strength that makes his story compelling. To most, his existence mystifies all reasoning, but as it is with any misunderstood creature, his origins cannot be explained until now.

To the surprise of most, the creature known as Bigfoot wasn't always a Bigfoot. Initially, he was a man, and like most of humanity, he possessed a name. Before receiving his designation as Bigfoot, the creature was once known as Quincy Pendergast.

This young man hailed from the eastern shores of the mighty Mississippi. His family's farm was situated south of the Rock River where it joins the mighty river on its journey south towards the Bayou. His childhood was spent laboring in the fields of his family's five-hundred-acre farm. Of the many things the Pendergasts grew, it was their distinguished crops of radishes that gave them the most recognition.

For Quincy, picking radishes was never an option. Between their texture and the surplus of radish-based meals that he's digested over the years, Quincy has looked for any opportunity that would lead him away from his family's farm. His willingness to leave was not solely driven by his disdain for the over-consumption of radishes, rather he grew tired of his four older brothers.

Being the youngest of five, Quincy had been picked on his entire life. Unfortunately for him, he grew to be quite short even for his age. By the time he had reached eighteen years old, he would often be mistaken as a child of thirteen rather than the young man he was.

Due to this inconvenience, Quincy was forced to look up to his four older brothers rather than uncover what was ahead. As is the case with anyone who is caught looking away from the obstacles in front of them, Quincy was exposed to the very things that would cause him to stumble. Regrettably, his mother was no solace of comfort. She often stated his shortcomings by reminding Quincy of her desire for him to be more like his brothers.

It was a lonely way to go through life. Quincy seemed to fail at everything he did. What made matters worse was that his family began placing no expectations on him. They viewed him as someone who would never achieve anything. On occasion, the four brothers could be found arguing amongst themselves over who would get stuck taking care of him. Each one believed Quincy was going to need their help through the remainder of his life.

While his four brothers tussled over this pending reality, their resentment towards him grew. Each day provided his brothers with new opportunities to mock and torment him. Quincy couldn't remember the last time he found relief inside his family's farm. He believed his days there were numbered.

For Quincy, there was no way to continue living in that manner. Six months after his eighteenth birthday, Quincy decided to step off his family's farm and set out to prove himself as a man. However; the more accurate statement would be, "He took off to prove himself to his family."

The problem when undertaking such a task is there aren't many ways in which someone can prove themself as a man. Quincy traveled east towards the great city of Chicago, hoping to find a line of work that would fit his needs. Before he stepped off the train, Quincy understood there wasn't much of a chance of finding such a job, or any other job for that matter. It was the era of The Great Depression and for an eighteen year old the world's problems seemed far away. These issues seemed small and insignificant to Quincy, that is until these problems became his own.

While in Chicago, he spent every day outside the postal office hoping to find work. On the side of the building hung a bulletin board that allowed businesses to list available jobs. After spending a week in the city, Quincy began to understand his error in this decision.

On the day he was about to return home, a sign appeared which grabbed his attention. Since he arrived in Chicago, Quincy became accustomed to the ritual of men cheering over each posting. The cause of this routine has developed over time and is the result of men becoming familiar with one another. Their acquaintances with each other have allowed them to know who was best suited for the day's posting. There is a chorus of cheers that would follow each

prospective victor as he left his comrades, but not this morning. This morning aroused a different kind of reaction. Instead of excitement, the crowd began to murmur over the morning's posting. As he approached the board, Quincy overheard a few of them utter, "The nerve of that guy."

Being curious, Quincy was driven to see what the fuss was about. He uncovered that the bulletin board announced a job out in the Cascade Mountains. As he further inspected the poster, he came across the phrase, "Lumberjacks Wanted." Below these bold words was another sentence that read, "Real Men Can Wield an Ax!"

Quincy thought, "This is it!" The words on this poster illuminated Quincy's soul. He knew that by proving himself as a lumberjack his brothers would have to accept him. There's no way they would make fun of him when he showed how skilled he was with the tool. He thought, "If I could tear down one tree, I know I can stand up to them."

As soon as he could, Quincy left Chicago and made his way out to the Cascades. On his trip west, Quincy regularly pulled out his ax to practice his swings. Every night he volunteered to chop wood for the fire. By the time he reached the base camp near Mount Bachelor, Quincy was certain he could best any lumberjack on the mountain.

Unfortunately, no amount of practice would help him overcome his stature. He still looked younger than any other eighteen-year-old on the mountain. Once he was out of the truck, Quincy realized the torment he faced from his brothers was not exclusive to them. There was no way of hiding from this truth once the foreman laid eyes on him. Quincy could see that his recently acquired dream of becoming a lumberjack was now in jeopardy.

The foreman, an older man in his fifties, looked Quincy over. There wasn't a slight hesitation in his demeanor. The foreman's first reaction when seeing Quincy was to laugh and laugh is what he did. He bellowed from the bottom of his belly and shook himself so badly that he needed to stabilize his frame by grabbing his left knee. He stopped laughing long enough to exclaim, "Son, I can't do anything with you. Some of my men's legs are bigger than you!"

"Please sir, I know I can do this," begged Quincy, "give me a chance."

The desperation in Quincy's plea allowed the foreman to take pity on him. He had never seen anyone as dismal as Quincy appear at that moment. Instead of dismissing him, the foreman agreed to hire him based on one condition. He explained, "Son, I can't put you up in those trees with an ax. Besides, we're likely to get one of those new saws everyone is talking about. I've never seen one, but I've heard they're pretty heavy. If I put you up in a tree, you're likely to kill someone. Give it time though. If you work hard enough around camp, I'll see if I can find you a spot on top."

Upon hearing this offer, Quincy's disposition changed. His solemn demeanor had dissolved and was replaced with a youthful zeal. His mood changed so much that it caused him to shake his fists frantically in the air. Without hesitation, he went around the camp performing every task that was assigned to him.

His duties consisted of sharpening the tools, sweeping the bunkhouses, and picking up every piece of trash around the camp. Additionally, after every meal he was required to help the camp's cook in cleaning the mess hall. Although he hated the work, Quincy believed it was worth the effort. Anytime he doubted this, he simply reminded himself, "Whatever it takes to wield an ax."

Sadly, working hard wasn't enough for Quincy. He quickly learned a harsh truth of life, 'people see only what their eyes permit them to see'. This limitation is another challenge that each person faces when they're required to overcome their prejudices. For Quincy, he could never escape his size, the others in camp wouldn't allow him.

At first impression, Quincy's coworkers were dismissive of him. Their attitudes then evolved into annoyance as they watched him tirelessly work around the camp. Finally, they settled into amusement. The other loggers took it upon themselves to make his duties as difficult as they could. They twistedly enjoyed watching his shoulders shrink each day as they caused him more problems around the camp.

A select few have gone out of their way to make the camp messier than usual. This awful act was done to provide themselves with a few laughs for the day. Their efforts went further by performing horrible tricks at Quincy's expense. They never passed on an opportunity to slop grease on his broom handle or stuff rocks in his shoes.

Despite this torment, Quincy did his best to reign in his emotions. However, each time the crew ascended the mountain, he found himself tightening his grip on the broom's handle. By nighttime Quincy could feel how depleted his energy was. Rather than quit, he understood the consequences of going back to his family's farm. That pending reality is the only thing that kept him committed to his duties.

Unfortunately; the crew found the one thing that could break his spirit. In the past, his brothers assigned him a terrible nickname and somehow that name found its way into the camp. Quincy believed the nickname "Incy Quincy" behaved more like a leech possessing predatory intent rather than some mocking phrase.

Quincy had enough. He wanted to believe the foreman would give him his chance, but on most days he never noticed him. He understood that the only way he could move forward was to grab his ax and cut down the tallest tree he could find. Afterward, the foreman would have to notice him.

At night, Quincy constructed his plan of action and went through the camp pilfering any item he needed for the next morning. He concluded that it was vital for him to leave early enough, so he could avoid anyone seeing him. If spotted, they may try to stop him.

As the next morning arrived Quincy grabbed his things and snuck out of the camp. Since being hired on; Quincy had heard a few of the men discussing a monstrous tree near the ridge of the mountain. Supposedly, a couple of the men had tried to chop it down, but the bark was so thick that it split their axes in two. Word spread and it was determined that the location of the tree made it difficult to haul any of its frame away, leading the foreman to the conclusion of letting the tree be.

Before setting off, Quincy recalled this story and determined that it was the only tree for him. If he was ever going to get the respect he required, it would take a tree like that to do so. He pulled down his cap and set out, searching for this behemoth.

With each step up the mountain, Quincy took notice of the air. Every hundred feet he went, it became lighter and cooler. The ascent into the mountain caused his lungs to burn. Quincy seemed to struggle with every breath he took.

While he attempted to collect as much air as possible, Quincy failed to account for the effect the air was having on his cheeks. Calluses formed on the skin, tightening the area around his cheekbone. Additionally, the frigid air found a way to crack his bottom lip. It wasn't until the sun peeked over the mountain's edge that his waxed expression melted away, allowing him to find full movement of his face again.

Thankfully, once the sun pierced the sky, Quincy found it! A hundred yards away, in the clearing, was the biggest tree he'd ever seen. He hurried as quickly as his legs would carry him.

Once at the base of this tree, he couldn't believe how it stretched into the sky. It's as if the tree was the only thing capable of matching the mountain in size.

While walking around its base, Quincy struggled to account for his steps. Several times he stumbled over the outstretched roots. It didn't help that he took his eyes off of where he was going. Distracted by the sheer size of the pending foe who remained grounded in front of him.

After taking a couple of laps around its base, Quincy tried to count the amount of steps he took when encircling the trunk. He lost track after fifty. Instead of wasting further time on measuring its base, Quincy shifted his focus to locating a branch that would help him scale this tree.

The lowest branch he found was still three feet from his reach. Refusing to give up, Quincy grabbed several rocks. After piling them on top of each other, Quincy navigated his way to the top of his makeshift mountain, yet he was still short of the branch. It seemed to him that no matter what he did he couldn't reach the limb.

After taking a couple of laps around its base, Quincy tried to count the amount of steps he took when encircling the trunk. He lost track after fifty. Instead of wasting further time on measuring its base, Quincy shifted his focus to locating a branch that would help him scale this tree.

The lowest branch he found was still three feet from his reach. Refusing to give up, Quincy grabbed several rocks. After piling them on top of each other, Quincy navigated his way to the top of his make-shift mountain, yet he was still short from the branch. It seemed that no matter what he did he couldn't reach the limb.

Right then a brisk breeze rolled through the branches. To Quincy, he was certain the sound coming off the rustling needles was that of laughter. It's as if the tree was enjoying his failure. Again the wind blew through the tree causing the same sound. This time Quincy heard his brothers, mocking him once more.

Although angry, his frame was depleted. Between his climb up the mountain and failing in his latest attempt at the tree, Quincy's body seemed to give up. He sat down on one of the roots and sobbed for some time.

When his tears dried up, Quincy concluded, "Maybe everyone's right, I am 'Incy Quincy'". He slunk back into the tree, hoping that it would somehow envelop him into its frame. He knew his chance of proving himself was slipping away and there was nothing he could do about it.

It's at this time, between outbursts, that Quincy caught sight of a light flashing below him. Initially he took no thought of it. Instead of pursuing the source of this light, he chose to focus on his pain. Again, a single flash of light broke his concentration. Rather than ignore the flicker, Quincy attempted to spot where it was coming from.

After clearing his eyes of any lingering tears, Quincy turned his attention to a meadow located below the tree. While squinting he assumed, "It must be a pond or something."

Instead of wallowing away in pity, Quincy thought it was best to search for the source of this light. To his surprise it wasn't a pond or some piece of metal in the clearing. No, it was a flower! A single golden flower.

Right then a brisk breeze rolled through the branches. To Quincy, he was certain the sound coming off the rustling needles was that of laughter. It's as if the tree was enjoying his failure. Again the wind blew through the tree causing the same sound. This time Quincy heard his brothers, mocking him once more.

Although angry, his frame was depleted. Between his climb up the mountain and failing in his latest attempt at the tree, Quincy's body seemed to give up. He sat down on one of the roots and sobbed for some time.

When his tears dried up, Quincy concluded, "Maybe everyone's right, I am 'Incy Quincy'". He slunk back into the tree, hoping that it would somehow envelop him in its frame. He knew his chance of proving himself was slipping away and there was nothing he could do about it.

It's at this time, between outbursts, that Quincy caught sight of a light flashing below him. Initially, he took no thought of it. Instead of pursuing the source of this light, he chose to focus on his pain. Again, a single flash of light broke his concentration. Rather than ignore the flicker, Quincy attempted to spot where it was coming from.

After clearing his eyes of any lingering tears, Quincy turned his attention to a meadow located below the tree. While squinting he assumed, "It must be a pond or something."

Instead of wallowing away in pity, Quincy thought it was best to search for the source of this light. To his surprise, it wasn't a pond or some piece of metal in the clearing. No, it was a flower! A single golden flower.

Quincy didn't think much of the flower, his focus remained on that tree. However, as he stepped away from its trunk, there was something about the flower that kept his attention.

As he came closer, Quincy could see that the flower's petals had been infused with colors of red, orange, and yellow. Giving it the most unique look he's ever seen.

Stunned by its presence, Quincy looked to see if there were any other flowers like it. Strangely, not only were there no other flowers like it, there weren't flowers of any kind around. Somehow this flower was isolated, alone, on top of this range. To Quincy, it seemed unlikely that this or any flower could have survived in this frigid climate, yet there it was. Quincy had to see what made this flower so special.

He bent down and inspected the flower from pedal to pedal. At first glance, the flower didn't seem special. Other than the infused colors and isolation, nothing seemed different about it.

Wishing to learn more, Quincy leaned closer, smelling the flower. Its fragrance issued a splendid odor that he couldn't recognize. The scent was so unique that he sniffed as much as his nose could manage. A funny thing happened, Quincy inhaled so much that a batch of pollen flew up his nose, causing him to sneeze.

As he sneezed a tiny fairy appeared in front of him, choosing to sit on one of the pedals. Although the fairy couldn't be bigger than his thumb, Quincy could make out some things from this figure. Her hair was a shade of auburn; which seemed to capture the light of the sun, making it difficult to focus on her whereabouts. Although small in stature, her figure resembled that of his mother.

Confused at the sight of the fairy, Quincy sat and stared. It was the fairy who first spoke, "What are you doing here?

Quincy could ask it the same thing, but instead answered, "I'm here to chop down this tree."

"Why would you want to do that?" asked the fairy.

"To prove that I'm a man," replied Quincy.

"That's a silly reason," remarked the fairy.

"You're one to talk. You're nothing, but a silly little fairy. You're probably not even real," mocked Quincy.

"I am too real!" yelled the fairy, "and to prove it I'll give you one wish."

"One wish? Can you do that?" asked Quincy.

"Of course! Anything magical can grant one wish," explained the fairy.

"Why one?" asked Quincy

"There's only enough magical power in this flower for one wish, after it's given it'll have to be planted somewhere else," the fairy added.

"So the flower is the one with the power?" questioned Quincy.

"Not exactly... we're the same, the flower and me. The flower gets its power from me and I from it. By granting a wish, a part of that power is gone; lost somewhere in the soil. So I'll have to move on and find a new place to plant it," shared the fairy.

"If you have to move it, why grant me a wish in the first place?"

The fairy gave a faint smirk, far too subtle for Quincy to see. She answered, "I think it's time to move on. If people are coming up here to chop down trees for no reason, then it's time I find a new place to go."

"Alright, let's do this then," announced Quincy.

"Are you sure you know what you want?" asked the fairy.

"Without a doubt," proclaimed Quincy, " I've been picked on my entire life and I'm ready to wish for the one thing that will make it all stop. I wish to be taller and stronger than any man, that I'll be big enough that people will have to respect and fear me. If I had that, then maybe people would finally leave me alone."

Sorry to hear of his woes, a part of the fairy wanted to spare Quincy from the wish he was about to make. She questioned, "Are you sure that's what you want?"

"Yes I'm sure, my whole life I've been picked on and I want everyone to leave me alone," declared Quincy.

A sudden flash came out of the flower. By the time Quincy adjusted his eyes, both the fairy and flower were gone. Curious to see whether he hallucinated the whole thing, Quincy looked around hoping to find something that would indicate to him that it was real. Unfortunately, everything seemed the same. Annoyed and disappointed by the outcome, Quincy decided it was time to go back to camp.

It was mid-day when Quincy returned. Everyone there had already left for the woods. Rather than sulk, Quincy determined it was best for him to go back to his duties. In the mess hall was the broom along with the mop and bucket. A strange thing happened when Quincy went to retrieve them; he couldn't fit through the door. Quincy tried a different angle to see if that would let him in, but it was no use.

Confused, Quincy did his best to figure out what was going on. He then recalled his wish and thought, "Is it possible? Did my wish come true?" He had to see himself in a mirror. He ran to the bathroom, but couldn't fit in.

While in the camp he began pacing back and forth, contemplating his next move. "My cot," he muttered, "I know how big my cot is, if I lay in it then I'll know."

He raced towards his tent, but as he attempted to unbutton the flaps, Quincy noticed his fingers. Somehow they were different. Now they're hairy! As he fumbled the buttons through his fingers, Quincy could hear someone coming back towards the camp. He rushed over to see who it was.

Pretty soon the person came into sight, it was the foreman! Quincy remembered how he often returned to camp once he squared away the other lumberjacks. Of the hundred people nestled in this camp, it was the foreman Quincy had hoped to see.

He sprinted towards him believing the foreman would confirm his suspicion, possibly setting him up in one of the trees with the rest of the crew. Once Quincy had passed the mess hall, the foreman spotted him. His face fell in terror. Quincy stopped running, fearing that something ferocious was following him.

When he turned to look behind him, the foreman began creeping away so as not to alarm Quincy. After reviewing the surrounding area, Quincy couldn't see anything that would cause the foreman to freeze in that manner. He turned back towards him and saw the foreman was attempting to walk away.

Quincy took one step forward and the foreman yelled, "Stop! Don't come any closer. I'm warning you!"

Quincy thought he was joking. As he continued walking towards him, the foreman reached down and picked up a fallen branch and held it as if it were an ax. If there was one thing the foreman knew how to do, it was to wield an ax. Quincy stopped.

He decided it was best to talk to the foreman instead. He began, "Greeaguaguea." "What was that?" he thought.

He tried once more, "Buaaawguaagh."

Nonsense? Quincy was speaking nonsense. Frustrated, Quincy roared. His bellowing voice rolled through the mountain range alarming the other lumberjacks. Fearing the worst they climbed down from their perches and rushed back towards the camp.

As Quincy continued shouting in his newly formed tongue, the foreman crouched into a ball, covering his ears from the thunderous noise reverberating from Quincy's throat. By the time he finished belting out his frustrations, the crew had arrived and then dropped to the forest floor in disbelief at what they saw.

Some of the crew fell back, pleading to God, hoping he would spare them from this terrible beast. As Quincy examined their reaction, he knew the fairy's magic had worked. He recounted the wish he made and remembered that he had wished to be taller and stronger than any man. He pressed his thoughts, searching for any other aspect of the wish that he might've missed. He then remembered wishing to be respected and?

It took a moment, but Quincy realized he wished that everyone would be afraid of him. He looked at the cluster of men cowering before him and understood how that last portion of the wish changed him into whatever he'd become.

"What did she do to me?" he questioned.

What indeed? Without knowing the consequences he would face for wishing such a wish, Quincy shot up in size, he towered over everyone in the camp. Without measuring tape, no one could be certain how tall Quincy was. He appeared to be over seven feet tall. His face and body were now covered in hair. Instead of being able to explain himself, all his coworkers could hear was his deafening roars.

The noise spewing from his mouth twisted their stomachs and weakened their knees. Soon one of the men spoke up and said, "Men, what are we doing? Why are we standing here with our axes like little children, let's stand like men and take down this beast!"

Another voice shouted, "He's right, there's a hundred of us and one of it! Why should we be afraid? Let's kill it before it kills us!"

Not a single voice opposed these suggestions. The group of lumberjacks jumped to their feet and cheered in unison. Stunned by this sudden revelation, Quincy knew he had one option left, so he ran. He ran as fast as his legs would carry him.

Remarkably, he was quite agile for his new size. His body carried him farther and higher than any woodsman was willing to go. Once they were out of sight, he stopped and recognized where he was. Below him was the tree he attempted to cut down earlier that morning. He walked back towards the meadow where he first saw the flower.

Once there, Quincy begrudgingly admitted that the flower had already moved on. Instead of giving up, he pressed towards the meadow, hoping the fairy was teasing him; possibly teaching him a lesson. When the meadow came into sight, there wasn't a single sign of the flower.

Quincy dropped to the ground and wept in agony. His short existence on earth has been layered with all forms of teasing and torment, and now this! In all his life he'd never imagined doing something so stupid. He lay down next to where the flower once was, looking up towards the sky. While underneath the noonday sun, Quincy reflected on his choices. He wondered why he ever left his home. Quincy twisted his thoughts on those things he'd miss. His agitation grew so heavily that his entire frame shook the ground beneath him. As his body lay where it was, Quincy mourned for his lost life. He skulked as he watched the sun cross the sky.

Once night fell, Quincy could feel drops of rain beating against his forehead. With nowhere else to go, he decided his best bet for shelter was the tree he attempted to cut down earlier that day. He stayed there, underneath its outstretched branches, and fell into a deep slumber.

The next morning, with the rising sun beating against his back, Quincy awoke to find a pond where the meadow once was. The last day went by so quickly that Quincy didn't realize he had ignored his body's pleas for food and water. The sight of the pond reminded him of how thirsty he was.

While kneeling near its edge Quincy buried his face into the mountain water. After engulfing as much water as his body could take, Quincy sat there, placing his hands on his lap trying to figure out what was next.

Once the ripples settled in the pond, Quincy saw what the fairy had done to him. He fell back from the water in shame. Until that moment, he never considered how disfigured his face had become.

He knew there was no way for him to go back to the world of men. He would either be hunted or studied once discovered. Unfortunately, his best course of action was to remain hidden, within the trees.

That's when a thought reached his mind, "The fairy. She did this, she could undo it! She never said I was given just one wish."

A sense of purpose crept in. If anyone could fix what's been done, it's her. Quincy's now convinced that the fairy could save him.

With a firm sense of resolution as his guide, Quincy set himself out to uncover the whereabouts of the golden flower. Finding one flower in a world as big as ours isn't an easy task to undertake. Some have seen Quincy wandering here and there. Others are convinced he's a myth. Yet, to this day, Quincy is still searching to undo that thing that has been done.

Michael J. Egbert started his writing career developing marketing and communication strategies for small businesses. His love for writing began at his alma mater, Utah Tech University where he studied human communication. Michael continued his education by enrolling in a master's program at the University of Southern California Annenberg, School of Communication and Journalism.

Michael is married to his college sweetheart, Delight. Together they reside in Las Vegas, Nevada, with their three children.